BG

D0606111

McCrephy's Field

CHRISTOPHER A. MYERS AND LYNNE BORN MYERS

Illustrated by Normand Chartier

HOUGHTON MIFFLIN COMPANY

BOSTON 1991

For Rae, Mickey, Dorothy, and Roscoe
— C. A. M. and L. B. M.

As always, for Molly and Sam
— N. C.

Library of Congress Cataloging-in-Publication Data

Myers, Christopher A.
  McCrephy's field / written by Christopher A. Myers and Lynne Born
Myers ; illustrated by Normand Chartier.
      p.   cm.
  Summary: Relates how the plants and animals around a farmer's barn
change over the course of fifty years.
  ISBN 0-395-53807-6
  [1. Nature—Fiction. 2. Barns—Fiction.] I. Myers, Lynne Born.
II. Chartier, Normand, 1945–   ill. III. Title.
PZ7.M9824Mc 1991   90-39054
[Fic]—dc20   CIP
                           AC

Text copyright © 1991 by Christopher A. Myers and Lynne Born Myers
Illustrations copyright © 1991 by Normand Chartier

Printed in the United States of America

HOR   10 9 8 7 6 5 4 3 2 1

Joe McCrephy was a farmer who grew corn in Ohio. He grew his corn in long, neat rows. When Joe was twenty-four, he left his cornfields to help his brother raise goats in Wyoming. This is the story of what happened to Joe's field while he was away.

Joe left in the fall. Because he had not planted corn that year McCrephy's field was bare, except for the earthworms under the ground, and maybe a spider and a beetle or two. Mice scurried in the large red barn and hid grains of corn in the toe of one of Joe's old galoshes.

Winter came, and snow fell on McCrephy's field. The ground was very white and very empty. A red-tailed hawk flew over, but he found nowhere to rest and nothing to eat, so he flew on. The mice in the barn slept through the cold.

When spring arrived, McCrephy's field blossomed with hundreds of flowers. There were Queen Anne's lace and buttercups; shepherd's purse and sweet peas; Indian paintbrush and asters.

Next grew goldenrod, pigweed, cocklebur, and oxeye daisies.
Butterflies and bumblebees drifted lazily in the warm sun.
McCrephy's field filled with the songs of meadowlarks.

By fall, McCrephy's field had turned ragged. The petals had dropped from the flowers, and the stalks hung heavy with seed. Honeysuckle and blackberries grew in tangled heaps. Some trees had started to grow, but they were no taller than a man's knee. Field sparrows and goldfinches came to feast on the bounty of seeds. Dry leaves and thistledown swept through the air.

After five years had passed, there were many more trees in McCrephy's field — some as tall as a man. A family of cottontail rabbits made a home beneath the blackberry bushes, and there were skunks near the wild roses.
A praying mantis fed mostly on grasshoppers.

After ten years, McCrephy's red barn began to turn gray
with age. There were trees all over the field. Some were
almost as tall as the barn. There was no more Queen Anne's
lace or pigweed, because neither grows well in the shade.
Some violets and lady slippers appeared instead. The
meadowlarks left to build their nests in open pastures.
Cardinals and bluebirds moved in, because they like to nest
in the trees.

A red fox dug a den in the east end of the field,
and two box turtles lumbered nearby.

When twenty-five years had gone by, McCrephy's field
looked like real woods. There were walnut trees, sugar maples,
sassafrases, black cherry trees, mulberries, and oaks.

Two black oaks were larger than the barn and
had downy woodpeckers living in the trunks.
Small wildflowers like spring beauties,
bloodroots, and trout lilies sprouted on the
forest floor.

Fifty years had passed. All the older trees were now much taller than the barn, and there were smaller trees, like dogwood and redbud, flowering beneath them. In the midday heat, a small herd of white-tailed deer liked to rest in the cool shelter of the forest.

At night, a great horned owl hooted from her nearby nest.
An opossum climbed through the branches, carrying her
young on her back.

By day, a cooper's hawk swooped through the trees.

Joe McCrephy came back to Ohio in the summer to visit the land he had once farmed. He was now an old man. The field was not as he remembered it.

He walked through woods that were once long, neat
rows of corn. If not for the barn, he would not have
known it was his field.

"You and I have gone through some changes," he said to his field. He took out his penknife and carved his initials, *J.M.*, on the barn door. Then he lay down in the shade of a big red oak for a short summer nap.